P9-DMA-180

Merry Christmas

from

Johannes Fure

December 25, 2011

THE INVENTION OF LEFSE

"Lefse? What's lefse?"

REINGOLD KNEEBURR

T h e

INVENTION

o f

LEFSE

A CHRISTMAS STORY

LARRY
WOIWODE

:: CROSSWAY

Wheaton, Illinois

The Invention of Lefse: A Christmas Story

Copyright © 2011 by Larry Woiwode

Published by Crossway
        1300 Crescent Street
        Wheaton, Illinois 60187

All rights reserved. No part of this publication may be reproduced, stored in a retrieval system, or transmitted in any form by any means, electronic, mechanical, photocopy, recording, or otherwise, without the prior permission of the publisher, except as provided for by USA copyright law.

Interior illustrations: Noble Illustrations, Inc.

Cover illustration: Bridgeman Art Library, Joanne MacVey

Cover & interior design: Studio Gearbox

First printing 2011

Printed in the United States of America

Hardcover ISBN: 978-1-4335-2736-4
PDF ISBN: 978-1-4335-2737-1
Mobipocket ISBN: 978-1-4335-2738-8
Epub ISBN: 978-1-4335-2739-5

Library of Congress Cataloging-in-Publication Data
Woiwode, Larry.
The Invention of Lefse : a Christmas story / Larry Woiwode
     p. cm.
   ISBN 978-1-4335-2736-4 (hc)
   ISBN 978-1-4335-2739-5 (ebk.)
   1. Poor families—Norway—Fiction. 2. Christmas
stories.
   I. Title.
PS3573.O4I58   2011
813'.54—dc22   2011005642

Crossway is a publishing ministry of Good News Publishers.

LB   21   20   19   18   17   16   15   14   13   12   11
14   13   12   11   10   9   8   7   6   5   4   3   2   1

For Medora,
oldest grandchild

Mette's window was a porthole on the winter sky. The window was new since November, a gift from her papa. He toted the glass home from Oslo in a tin of sawdust. Then he sawed an opening in the logs of her loft and formed a frame of wood, perfectly circular, to hold the pane of glass. The window was as round as the portholes in a ship Mette saw when she traveled with her parents on the train to Oslo.

She said her morning prayers in bed, sunk in warmth, too Lutheran to callous her knees, her papa said. All was not well. A baby brother had not arrived again this year, though the family kept praying, and the crops were awful across the nation of Norway—independent now for two years. Their own wheat came in well enough, though, because of the gift of their valley, her pa said, but cousins and uncles laughed at the out-of-the-way woods where Mette and her family lived. Mette Iversdatter, her father's daughter.

On hot August days she and her pa watered their wheat with buckets carried from a ravine on shoulder yokes Papa carved. And in the evening, after a day's work, Mette had to read to her little sisters till they fell asleep.

"You must learn to read without error," her mother insisted. "You must be literate!"

Mette sat up, drawing her covers close, and scratched at a fuzz of frost on the window's edge, a wintry sound, forcing ice under her nails, though she kept them bit short, and sucked at the ice to wet her lips. Today the family had to travel to the Andrésons, Mette's mother's family, for Christmas Eve. Her papa's parents, from Trondheim, died when he was a boy. That was why they were fortunate, he said, to find this valley farm outside of either family.

The long ride to the outpost of the Andréson clan, near Bø, was the only trip they took—or took each Christmas since her pa built a sledge to carry them all. Mette could barely keep track of which trip was the last or which the one before, because the Andréson clan crowded the house with the noisy heat of their arguments, and cousins teased her about the woods.

She was thirteen, the reason she received a round window, her papa's gift for her birthday on November sixth.

She heard her parents below, whispering to keep their voices under control, but they were arguing. It wasn't because they didn't like each other, her ma said, anyway most of the time, and the worst Mette had seen was when they threw tomatoes at each other in the garden.

But something wasn't right between Grampy Andrus and Papa. It had to do with her mother, she thought, besides living in the woods so far from Bø. Mette was the oldest, so she understood the words her parents spoke, but she had to figure out their meaning for herself. After her came Andrusa, and then Kirsti, five and three—baby bawlers still.

She rose and made her bed and used the chamber pot, then pulled her wool work shift on over her nightgown, studying the ladder that led down. The family would leave early this year, her pa said, so there would be no talk about showing up in the dead of the night, like trolls, as Grampy always said, but even the porthole of her window didn't help tell the hour now. It was the misty winter season when the sun seemed a silver pan set too high, with streamers curling from its edges in the chilly morning light.

Once the sun was on its way west, though, and the sky had a chance to clear, in the thick deep of midnight blue Mette could follow the path of the moon out her window.

She stepped down the ladder rungs, her back to the room, and on the cold boards turned to see her ma sitting at their table beside a candle, her face in her hands. "We have no gifts to take," she murmured, turning toward the dark behind her. "And you know how Dad is."

"What do you mean, Ma?"

"O, you know, *Dad.*"

"Papa?"

"Mine and him there."

"*Your* dads?"

"Those two!"

"Both dads?"

"Two dads on a headlong course toward collision!"

"Yes, us," Papa said in his gentle voice out of the dark beyond the candle. "And I do know how your dad is, dear, I do. He wants gifts."

"You spent our earnings on fancy glass windows!"

Her papa had put up a pane in the kitchen, too, larger than Mette's, above the wood counter where her ma mixed bread. Once it was in, Mette's ma exclaimed, "It's like standing outside!" Now in the dim light Mette could see the bulk of her papa's back, draped in his horsehair coat, as he headed toward the door.

"Help grind wheat, Mette," he said in his easygoing way, and turned and smiled at her. "Good morning! We had a good crop, no? We'll take wheat and bread, what we have, as gifts."

Mette's ma revolved the circular upper stone of a pair on the counter, gripping a wood handle at the stone's edge, and Mette noticed frost below the kitchen window and on the logs and floor in a corner, an invasion that always dampened her ma's mood. Mette helped by pouring wheat into the center hole of the upper stone whenever her ma paused. They ground enough flour for a week by the time Papa returned from chores, and her ma poured it into the flour cupboard under her counter.

"Aren't we going to take it?" Mette asked.

"We'll think about that," her mother said.

Papa had a slatted bucket in the crook of an arm, frost sparkling on his blond-red beard. "Old cow, new milk," he said, as he did every morning, smiling at Mette. "I can't get over how it comes out so warm it smokes out there. We'll take the milk and flour. It was a bad year for crops near Bø."

"Old Jed," he said, and set the bucket, still steaming, on the table, and went out to hitch their gray-going-white, Old Jed, to the sledge her papa built five seasons ago.

Mette helped her ma pack the flour into a wooden box Papa built last week, and then Mette and her mother covered it with diamond-patterned silk, so it was presentable as a gift.

"So this is it," her mother said, and sniffed as if preparing to cry, and at that moment Papa came in the door. He grabbed his rifle from its corner, dug in a pocket of his coat, and held out a leather mitten, revealing a pair of brass tubes, rounded at their ends.

"Two bullets left," he said in his sad voice.

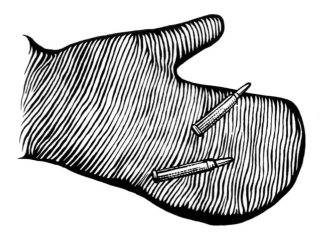

They packed up the sledge on wood runners, fitted with a box big enough to haul a load of hay or wood, or the five of them, every fixture of the sledge painted red and blue, except for the gold and green rosemaling on the back of its box—colors Mette loved. Her papa had laid a bed of straw in its box for warmth over the long ride ahead.

Mette followed her mother up the ladder to the attic, and from a trunk Papa had built they took out their Christmas dresses—traditional national dress, her mother once explained, only for special occasions; and now she explained it again, holding the dress against her front like a second person who had appeared, all smiles. They got into the dresses and went down the ladder and draped sheets over their shoulders, wrapping them around the dresses to keep them clean, and then pulled on their coats.

"Now the children," Ma said.

Both still slept in their parents' bedroom, such babies they abandoned their trundle bed at night and crawled in beside Ma and Papa. Both lay asleep in the center of the big bed. Mette and her mother dressed them as they slept, though Mette was sure Andrusa was pretending to sleep.

"Time to go!" Papa kept calling from outdoors.

It was a full day's ride to the Andrésons. Mette helped her mother settle the children and hopped in behind Pa's seat, wriggling into the straw beneath it, but with her head up high enough so she could see out. Her ma sank beside her and sighed, then lay back and smiled, staring at the silver sky.

"We're off," she whispered.

Old Jed nodded hard on the uphill trek out of the woods, hauling the load of them. But once on the flat above, he took off in his rocking, even trot, sending back the healthy horsey smell he gave off when he was busy at work for the family Mette knew he loved.

It was bare trees and evergreens and greener evergreens, the limbs of the biggest bowed with the weight of snow, no trail Mette could make out. Papa knew the way, of that she was sure, but at that moment he drew Jed to a halt and looked off to one side. Then he turned with a finger to his lips. Not far off Mette saw what seemed a pony with a pair of branches caught in its head, standing broadside to a huge evergreen, its nose raised and shining in the winter morning light.

The explosion of the rifle, echoing back from the hills by the time Mette recovered from the shock, sent Jed into a sideways lunge. The deer sprang and with a leap cleared the trunk of a downed tree.

"Missed!" her dad cried. "O, O, *O,* I was too anxious, too hungry, I was too much hoping I could bring the holiday feast! Meat enough for the winter, a buck that size!"

He laid his rifle behind the front board of the sledge and covered his face. "Gone!" He started to sob, clouts of breath clouding the air, his lips blubbering like rubbery bundles, bubbling the streamers from his nose.

"Your dad's on his way to an endless Norwegian night

of a black mood," Mette's mother whispered. "And this season he gets it bad."

Her mother waded through the straw on her knees and put her hands on his shoulders, then her arms around his neck. "Don't, Iver," she said. "Don't feel bad, shooting sitting from a sled! The next is ours."

"One shot left! And your dad will say, 'Did you bring me venison'—no he'll say deer meat—'Did you bring me deer meat from your woods?' And I'll be bound to say 'No, sir, I missed!'"

"We won't mention it, dear."

"He will! It'll be his first words!"

Mette's mother wiped at his face. "Don't," she said. "That will freeze and crack your cheek." She laughed. "Then what would I have to look at? You must keep the pace and get us there by dark."

Papa unhooked the reins from beside the seat, wiped his nose with the back of his mitten, and clucked and slapped the reins to set Jed off. But he kept hiccupping so hard Mette's mother, back beside her again, had to laugh a laugh she tried to cover with her mitten.

"I hear you back there," Papa said in his mournful voice.

By the time they reached a trail traveled by other sledges, Mette was so tired she dropped asleep. When she woke, points of stars shone in the winter violet, some gathered in such close clumps she could see red and gold and green streaks pulsing from the edges of silver. She heard her mother murmur and rose to see shining squares over sparkling snow—the windows of the Andréson place.

Mette clambered out, stiff from the cold, shocked wide awake by Papa clapping his leather mittens, so cold they clopped like wood. Mette and her ma gathered up the little ones, asleep again, while Papa set their gifts in the snow and unhitched Jed.

He led him toward the barn, past the stabbur, the place of celebration in Christmases past. Its narrow base and upper stories, with wide eaves on both sides, were packed with meats and food and frozen fruit and berries the cousins picked at, and then cavorted on all sides of the stabbur on skis and sleds. Uncle Orin rang the bell that in other seasons called the family from the fields for dinner, and scared off clouds of birds that nested above—the stabbur now empty, a hollow shell, her ma said, after the last long drought Grampy's farm went through.

A wooden door at the house groaned wide and Grammy Andréson stood outlined in a halo of light. "Ho!" she cried, "You're here already!"

She hurried out, a silver braid bouncing side-to-side below her bonnet, and took Mette's mother's hands. "Dear one," she said, and kissed her, and then, "O, dear, let me get this littlest girl, please. Then we'll hug!"

Mette's pa came crunching up and put the box of flour under one arm and the stoppered can of milk under the other, looking queasy.

Grammy turned and said, "The boys went to town and maybe got a jug because Daddy is acting like he's on a toot. We had bad news."

"Are they here?" a voice called from inside, and Grampy's face appeared at the door's edge, with his fringe of white beard and his white hair standing in spikes from his balding head in a blaze of light. "Is he here with my girl and grandkids? Yes, he is, and it ain't midnight troll time yet!"

Inside, in the pouring heat from the kitchen range, Mette smelled roast. "Uncle Benji stopped at the butcher in Bø," Grammy said to her, "and bought some cracklins, hog fat, so we saved one each for you.

Aunts and cousins in the kitchen stood staring at Mette and her family in the sidelong look that they might give beggars, Mette felt, and the faces of uncles kept appearing at different levels in the doorway to the sitting room.

Grampy clapped his hands and did a hop in his slippered feet. "So, sonny," he said to Mette's dad, "did you bring us deer meat?"

"No, sir, I missed," her pa murmured, and hung his head.

"*Missed?* What else more? My boys Lars and Orin, they come back from town, the store, with word of no more food on credit. How do I face the neighbors and trade folk in my shame? Who heard of a Norwegian who if he ain't rich got some few kronen hid away—worse, not even his credit no jimdamily good!"

He grabbed his beard in both hands and jumped up and down in the reindeer-leather slippers Mette's papa sewed for him last year. "And now no deer meat?" He pulled a pointy Santa cap with a white tassel off a wooden peg and jumped up and down on it. "What will Grampy do for Christmas! And his kids and relatives and grandkids, what'll *they* get?"

He trampled on the cap again, so short his waist barely rose above the kitchen table, a podgy gremlin, and when he hopped over to Mette she was surprised that she was taller and how his hug hit too low.

Mette's papa said, "We brought milk and flour, good wheat crop—"

"Oh, for—!" Grampy cried. "That's like hog slop. I meant food!"

"Ya, it's them," Uncle Benji with the big black beard said to the others in the sitting room at the center of the house. A rumble rose up.

"We thought maybe you forgot it was Christmas,

maybe," Uncle Lars, who still lived at home, said, squeezing past Benji, to Mette's papa.

"Like he maybe forgot about having sons," Orin, younger and still at home, too, stepped in and added, "Only daughters."

"Maybe he forgot how," a voice from inside the sitting room said, and the walls echoed with the laughter of a holiday crowd.

"I didn't think men could have sons," Mette's ma said, and Mette had to cover her mouth to keep from laughing at her clever reply.

"I might be a little guy," Grampy said. "But I make me big sons."

The crowd in the sitting room laughed again.

"So, Poppy-Grampy," Mette's mother said, a head taller than Grampy and holding him at arm's length after his hug, "you're on a toot?"

"Don't I wish!" He looked ready to hop again. "They did not let the boys have credit even on cheap boose. I ain't had a drink since Christmas last."

"Da-ad," Uncle Lars said.

"Well, maybe New Year."

"Da-ad."

"O, maybe a couple times this summer, I guess."

"Ya, more," Orin said.

"Shut up, boneheads! You're beholden to me to help! No boose, no snus, no deer meat, no kroner on credit with all that money I got in the bank!"

"Daddy!" Grammy said, and flipped back her braid. "Don't lie now."

"Or did once, yes. And look at this house, three big rooms and four bedrooms off them, enough loft to sleep the Swedish Army, our sitting room where once we held

dances for dozens to the Stavanger and squeezebox, yet now what we got? Naught! O how this house is fallen!"

"*O Daddy, Dad!*" rose from the adults in a tremolo that filled Mette with fear.

"On the other hand," he said, and slammed his palm. "We do not, like the Swedes, sell scythes to Lapps to cut hay for their reindeer when there ain't no grass in Lapland. We are honest and work hard for a crop every other five years or so from this god-blasted land!"

"Daddy!"

"*Da-ad!*"

"We tear fingernails off picking rocks! Ho, I'm checking, are you awake?" he said to Mette, chucking her under the chin. "We chop down trees to build barns or a stabbur—empty now!—and pick rocks in between, chopping down saplings that get going again, and then pick rocks yet once more from one end of the land to here—no fjord out front or fishing bay—and then pick the offspring, baby rocks that the rocks we picked had along the way, hunched over like this, backs all bent"—he waddled around Mette like a hunchback troll—"until we bang into a tree"—he rammed his head into the door frame, bending his sprouting hair—"because we forgot how the tree grew when we was busy picking rocks! Ja sure, to make sure not a stinker is left—you know how Norwegians are!"

"Poppy, don't bang your head again!"

"So is anybody better off in this land, including maybe especially this crybaby who misses his deer? I say to my boys, 'You boys, you move to America, so you can send home money real soon!'"

"I ain't!" Lars cried, and Grampy Andrus slapped the back of his head.

"Don't get highfalutin on me!" Grampy warned him.

"I shouldn't have missed," Mette's papa said.

"Why not? Why not one more worse thing? Okay, guys—you others, watch it, stand back!" he yelled at the faces gathered in the doorway. "You guys take off your wraps and come join our sobbing party on this crybaby Christmas Eve."

"Da-ad!"

"*Poppy!*"

"And don't go bawling in a corner about no deer."

"Daddy!"

Grampy Andrus strutted into the sitting room and said, "Ja, well, when you got an artsy-fartsy guy what spends a whole day building a box just-so square and then a week more puttering at painting it, you—"

"Dad!"

"I can't stand it," Grampy yelled, jumping up and down and looking for his Santa cap to jump up and down on. "I can't stand it, I can't stand I'm treated this way, I don't care who is at it! I want *credit*."

"He complains about as bad every Christmas," Grammy whispered in Mette's ear, her hands on Mette's shoulders gentle as her ma's.

"Ya, but we're so broke it's—" Grampy began, and then said, "Well, come on in, sit in heat, at least we got heat with all them trees."

He settled in his leather-bottomed rocker turned sideways to the fireplace, *the Klangstamp*, Mette's mother called it, because when Grampy finished it twenty years ago and sat down to test it, he realized one of its rockers was uneven, her ma said, with a knot in it, but refused to remove it and start over again.

Mette and her ma took a place on one of the benches around the walls of the sitting room, where uncles and cousins and aunts were seated—Bjørn and Sonja and Trygve and Selmer and Sigurd and Lena and Ole and Knut—in an atmosphere of pine pitch and burning birch and oak, lovely scents, Mette thought. At the far end of the room she saw, in a dimness that nearly hid it, a fir tree with colored rectangles dangling from its limbs. And then Mette's cousin Anna-Linne, older than Mette by two months, started chasing Andrusa around the room and Kirsti tried to keep up with them in the rocking run of a three-year-old, trailing her dress ties, already undone. At her mother's nudge Mette ran and tied them up.

"The Trondheim trolls will get you!" Uncle Ole yelled at the giggling, running girls, causing them to scream.

"The *Oslo* trolls!" Lars corrected.

"Ja, the politicians there," Grampy Andrus said.

"How free we been since we got our freedom?" Uncle Benji with the big black beard asked the roomful of folks, glancing around, eyes rolling.

"Well, we still got our rocks!" Grampy exclaimed, nodding at the fireplace, and the sniggering look of Benji and Lars suggested another meaning to Grampy's words. "But how far do they get you?"

Lars and Orin, on their bench at the side of the fireplace, crossed their legs at the same time, thoughtful, and each put a pipe in his mouth.

"No tobacco," Lars said, displaying his pipe to the room.

"We tried corn husks once," Orin said.

"Oofda," Lars said. "But I think I still taste some tobacco down here in mine."

"So what will this Storting in Oslo do next?" Uncle Benji asked.

"No more wars," Grampy said. "Let them Swedes go, like we did the Danes." He ran his hands over the standing-up hair that gave him the look of seeing a ghost. "We had too many wars already."

Uncle Lars stood and declaimed, "'Ten thousand Swedes ran through the weeds, chased by one Norwegian!'"

"Hush," Mette's ma said. "That is not nice."

"It sure is not news," Uncle Benji added.

"Isn't it time for prezies, giftie gifts, and that?" Grampy asked, and turned to Mette's mother. "What did you bring me?"

"Milk and fresh-ground flour, Dad, as Iver said."

"I like meat!"

Anna-Linne leaned to Mette, flushed and panting, and whispered, "Do you know I got me a new hope chest?"

"Yes," Mette said, and looked down. It was her hope for this Christmas.

After more back and forth about the cheerless season, Mette's mother took her hand and led her to the kitchen. "Ma," she said, "what do you have to cook? Daddy won't be happy till he eats."

"A few dozen potatoes black from getting bit by a freeze."

"Trim that off and set them boiling."

"Ya, we got plenty water with this snow."

"I'll make something heavy to fill him."

A sob came from Aunt Helge, Benji's wife, and she rolled her head on the wood counter where she sat. "Cracklins!"

she wailed. "And all I had to bring was a kerchief of sugar! What kind of gift is that?"

Aunt Hilde, next oldest to Mette's mother said, "I brought Norwegian flags I made of paper and painted for the tree, but no candles! We have hardly no food, too. We'll have to go on credit or butcher our cow. She's going dry anyhow from lack of fodder enough."

Aunt Magrete said, "I brought some dried-out old coffee beans. If you grind them up real fine you can imagine it tastes like coffee."

"Coffee!" Grammy cried. "I ain't had a cup in a month, only burnt barley at best—and ja, lots of that. *I'll* be on a toot!"

"Mette, skim off the top milk from our container and get Grammy's butter churn going," her ma said. "Butter's heavier than cream. I'll stir up a batter thick as steak with our flour and milk."

"Don't mention meat!" Hilde held her stomach that bulged so big Mette knew a baby rested in its infant's curl inside "Ma," she said, "there's hardly half our milk left. It must have spilled when Jed jumped at Papa's shot."

"Is cream on top?"

"Some, yes."

"Churn it."

Mette churned and churned, watching a pair of matching wooden paddles spinning inside a glass jar, and then hands that could only be her pa's had hold of her. "Honey, you're asleep." He lifted her and she felt his silky, giving beard soft on her cheek. "Time for bed."

He carried her to a corner, held up the sheet once encircling her dress as she changed to her nightgown, and then carried her to the sitting room, dim and quiet except for the fire, and settled her on a bench where her cousins slept.

Mette breathed in the summer aroma of heated pine, and said to her papa, "Will you tell me a story?"

"It's late, dear, and I'm feeling, O, so—"

"Bad?"

"Ja, but not so bad, either, now."

"Hey!" Grampy called. "Does big little Mette crave a story?"

"I asked Papa to tell me one."

"Get your skinny little body over here!"

"Da-ad!"

Mette's papa carried her to the rocker and set her in Grampy's smoky smelling arms. "I got a bushel of energy for all I don't eat," he said, starting to rock, *clang*, stamp! *clang*, stamp! "So open your ears to my story. Or are you too old? I don't know anymore how old you are, but you're big!"

"O, Grampy, you know."

"All my daughters, the three oldest, your ma especially,

liked these stories of mine, and knew when to give up sleep and sit for a story. So let me tell you the story of a girl, and I'll call her Mimi Obersdatter."

"Grampy, that's awfully close to me!"

"All my names are. It's about a girl, and the story is in Norway. Here, wait, before I go on you got to lean on my shoulder, there, like that. So now. Well, now, where was I going?"

"Mmm," Mette said, sleepy. "The story—"

"Mimi Obersdatter!"

"Mmm, close to me."

"She starts her morning in Norway at the century of my birth, the twenty-first, back in 1896—"

"Da-ad! That's later than I was born!" Lars exclaimed. "And that other is a—what do you call it? Anakrokism? It's a century not here yet!"

"It's a long story," Grampy said. "Use fantasy to imagine it. My granddaddy was alive at the time, the age you are now, Mette, and let's say you stand as you do at your round window and look out and see him. He's—"

"You know about my window?"

"O, I got spies. Your Pa made it for birthday thirteen, not?"

"You do know."

"So to Bø he went on his long trip after the harvest—

"Oslo."

"No kronen extra, and before he went, the story goes, he said, 'Ma, my peeping ears catch too much bedtime strife. Our big girl don't know how to rest with no way to look out on nature's gift.' So he gets the glass and makes the window, soaking the wood five days in the stream in the ravine so they bend just right and come out full round. Then painted it, I bet."

"Ja."

"'All our kronen on that!' the Ma of the house starts crying, once she sees it. 'And we not a speck of food. What'll we eat?'"

"Glass, Ma" he says, always the funny one, and you say it too.

"*Glass*," echoed from the walls around Mette.

"'*Well, okay, glass, then, and I tumble straight through to the ground*,' and Mette said, 'What's that?'"

"You fell asleep but see, you float! Who taught you that?"

"Ma."

"Not your papa."

"O, no, my pa, he lives life, no floating through."

"So! A pretty smart gal you think you are, no?"

"Only as much as I need for my good."

"Who taught you so?"

"Guess."

"Not your dad!"

"Both Ma and Papa."

"And now you want a story about trolls?"

"I don't think so."

"How's that!"

"The pagan past I don't admire."

"Is that right?"

"It's also my bedtime."

"Is that so?"

I don't like dreams of trolls, Mette thought, floating at a level below all this, feeling as sorry for Grampy as she would for anybody who never had her ma's teaching or Papa's wood-crafty workmanship outlook.

"And don't forget you're Norwegian."

"O, I know that!"

"It means you got to have fun. You got to run and play and sneak out in your woods and yell loud cough balls of *hey!* It means giving thanks."

"I'm myself when I don't think about my actions being mine—they run!"

"There is one I run to as heir of my wrongs and grammatapappies and yelling and the rest."

"I know."

"And what do I get?"

"Life."

"How'd you get so smart?"

"Ma teaching me."

"Ya, not your pa."

"He mostly lives it."

"How that hurts!"

Mette caught herself rolling off the bench beside the fireplace. So it was a dream, she thought, but wasn't sure. She remembered Grampy holding her in his rocker and talking about the window but she didn't know if he knew her papa put a round window in her upstairs attic room, and the rest was lost.

"Good morning, dear."

It was her mother, stirring up coals in the fireplace so Mette saw her face lit from below with red radiance. "We have a surprise for you."

"A present?"

"Yes, Christmas for you and the cousins who fell asleep before supper last night. Get dressed and come with me."

In the kitchen, aunts and uncles and cousins gathered on benches at a long wood table where the family ate, Grampy Andrus at the head on the far end, with Lars on his right and Orin on his left. Mette's ma lifted away an embroidered covering from a stack of pastry as round as pie crust but thinner and bigger than a pie. Grampy threw off the cover from a stack in front of him and flung one on his plate.

"Daddy!" Grammy cried, from Mette's end of the table. "You have to say grace! It's Christmas, you know."

Grampy held up both hands. "Grace!" he said.

The adults laughed and Mette's mother leaned and whispered to her, "It's a Norwegian thing."

Grampy held up a huge round of the pastry like a doily, gripping it with thumbs and fingertips, then ducked his head behind, and Mette saw it was browned across its surface in dappled spots. He peeked out, shook the pasty like cloth, and said, "This is all we need."

"Ya," Grammy said, "but I have a surprise." She walked over and set a pewter tankard beside Grampy's plate.

"This much lingonberry wine I saved back. You'll have to pass it, Andrus."

"Then I go last," Grampy said. "Or I'll guzzle so none's left."

"Don't I know," Lars said, and everybody laughed. Lars grabbed the tankard and took a slug and passed it on and when it came to Mette she glanced at her ma and her ma nodded. Mette took a sip and as its bitter sweetness slipped past her throat she felt a flash of heat from her crown to her toes. "O!" she said.

"Ya, you kids save some for me!" Grampy cried. "Here we go!" He held out his hands to Lars and Orin and everybody up and down the table joined hands and chanted:

Come, Lord Jesus,
Be our guest!
And let these gifts,
To us be blessed!

The stack in front of Mette, the one at Grampy's end, and another at the center of the table went gliding onto plates by way of fingers and forks.

"What is this?" Mette asked

"We didn't know what to call it," her mother said, "so Grampy—"

Grampy picked up from her and said, "I told them it lefs tha tathe in my mouf, which was full, so they said, 'Let's call it *lefse*!' So that's how it got its name and I named it!"

"What does it mean?"

"It means you're going to eat it!" Grampy said. "Butter it good. Sprinkle on a little sugar, roll it, like this. Eat it like a sausage! That's it!"

"Mmm, Mama, I never tasted anything like it. It tastes something like potatoes partly burned and—"

"Those are *ours!*" Grampy shouted.

"But not quite," Mette said. "It tastes like Christmas food should."

"It is Christmas, dear, and you're eating *lefse*. I used what we had in the house to make it." And then she whispered to Mette, "'*Out of their poverty came riches that abounded to many.*'"

"Ja!" Grampy said. "It was your flour and milk and butter, plus my potatoes, by golly!"

"And my sugar!" Helge yelled.

"Thanks for the churning, dear," Mette's ma said. "We found it is best with butter, and then sugar over that."

"Oh, *yes!*" the cousins cried.

"Let's have lefse every Christmas!" Grampy yelled, with shreds of the concoction fluttering from his lips, and then he pounded the table with both fists, one gripping a knife, the other a half-eaten lefse roll.

"*Yes!*" the cousins agreed.

"What an invention, Ma!" Mette said.

"For those who missed last night," Grampy said, "which was when we open gifts, since we had none, we had lefse instead. Now again!"

"Did Santa Claus come?" Mette asked, and her cousins laughed.

"No, dear," her mother said, and then to the table, "She knows"—and the cousins grew downcast and glum as swiftly as they had laughed.

Mette had been praying for a hope chest like the one Anna-Linne's parents got her a year ago in Oslo, and a wash of salt stung her eyelids.

"Lefse is the gift for all!" Grampy cried.

Mette's ma smiled and bit her lip as she did when she felt bad or held a secret back. To Mette and Andrusa, she said, "I'm sorry I have to say your pa has been out to hitch Jed to the sledge. We have to leave the minute we're done if we're to be home by dark."

"Grampy," Mette said. "Did you tell me a story last night?"

"I tried but you was sleepy. And, say, after you children was in bed, I think maybe Benji found a bitty bottle in a back pocket after all."

The grownups all laughed.

"Just a nip!" Grampy said. "But I been in such a holiday mood ever since! Lefse is why, too. And that name I give it! It's because I'm such a happy, holiday, inventive guy, I guess."

Mette hated to leave the families she wouldn't see for another year. Most of them lived not far from Grampy's but too far from their farm to visit. So it was goodbye to all of this, the cousins and uncles and aunts, the heat and noise and commotion of the family, and Mette bit into her lower lip to hold back tears. But when Grammy took her in a hug and Grampy hopped over to hug her, too, a burn like Oslo's bitter sea squeezed past her eyes and spilled and ran. At the sight of her tears, her mother started crying and Papa was hiccupping so badly he dashed out the door.

"Goodbye!"

Their painted sledge looked to Mette like a slice of spring in the winter morning light. She helped her ma bed the children down, and then worked herself deep into the straw, facing the rear instead of the front.

"Goodbye."

"*Bye!*"

By the time Jed evened out in his jogging trot, Mette was asleep.

The dream returned, a troll at her window, a fall from its height, but the stop this time was real. She sat to blue dark surrounding her, below a stand of mountain laurel where the sledge sat stilled. Whose woods they were she did not know but knew they were not theirs. Then her pa rose into view a ways away from Jed, his rifle raised as if pointed at the horse's ear, and Mette felt her mother's gentle hand on her shoulder. *"Shh."*

The flash came first with a sound like the worst breaking up of ice, and again Jed jumped. But Papa grabbed his bridle to hold him in check. "This one I got!" he cried. "He's bigger than the one I missed! Meat for the winter for all of us, a big fat buck! I can take your folks a quarter when I sell the wheat we talked about last night, so they have credit at the store. Mette, you come, too! You're old enough to help me drive to Bø."

Her ma and papa dressed the deer where it lay, exclaiming over its size and weight, the food supply they would store in a freezer box outside—snowbanks bloodied all around, steaming innards strewn aside in the cold for scavengers of the woods. Mette slipped down in the straw but kept a hold on the words of her pa—*old enough to help me drive.*

Old Jed shied at the smell of the quarters they carried

up, wrapped in oilcloth Papa kept in the sledge, and off they went. Mette tried to sleep but was jostled at every bump and curve by a lukewarm haunch of venison.

It was dark when they reached their valley, down its series of hills, with no welcoming glow from the house. It would be dead cold inside, as Papa put it, but the moon was out. "Look," he said, pointing. "I guess she must be full tonight."

"I think that was last night, dear. The children."

"Yes."

Mette asked if she could stay up and talk about their visit, the time with the relatives, to see if she had them straight—and Grampy, and lefse.

"No," her papa said, in his stern voice. "We have butchering to do. You go straight to bed."

Mette climbed the rungs of the ladder to her upstairs loft, and first she saw the window, which she sometimes felt she dreamed, and then a bulky, shadowy addition. On the floor below, lit by the moon and stars, was the hope chest she had prayed for, the buds and vines of rosemaling on its lid the loveliest her pa had painted, entwining a scrolled "M" at the center.

"Papa!" she cried.

His head was above the hatch her ladder poked through.

"Well, ja, I had a chance to carry it up when you were fussing with the little girls' dresses. Now you have a place to keep yours separate."

"O, Papa!" Mette ran and fell to her knees and set her hands to both sides of his beard, as she'd seen her mother do, and kissed him on the mouth.

"O, ah, *thanks*," he said, and wiped his lips, surprised.

"Your Ma traced out the rosemaling pattern for me to paint. We couldn't give it at Grampy's, knowing everybody had so little."

"Thank you both!"

"Yes, dear," her mother said, her face appearing beside Papa's as he grabbed her around the waist with an arm. "And there's one more detail. Your dad meant it when he said you had to sleep now, Mette, dear, but we want you to know, as oldest, that a brother will be with us when the snow is gone. This one doesn't swim like you nice girls but kicks hard as a horse."

"O, Mama!" Mette took her mother's face in her hands and kissed her on the mouth, too. "I can't wait!"

"Well, we must," her mother said. "It's the rule."

"Rest now, dear," Papa said, and Mette kissed them each one time more, goodnight kisses.

In the moon and starlight she removed her holiday dress, folded it and placed it at the bottom of her chest, rich with the scent of newly sawed wood. She smiled at the thought of her tears and her ma's favorite saying, "Never misjudge a Norwegian."

Mette drew on her nightgown, got into bed, and performed a sideways swim to the center of the covers. Heat was already rising from the fire in the kitchen below, and beneath its breathy, crackling sounds she could hear, through the boards of her floor, the sound of her parents' pleasant voices as they worked, and then laughter.

Meat enough for the winter! Help to Papa driving to Bø! Her window and a hope chest! Plus the invention of lefse! But best was a brother on the way. In a blur she said her evening prayers before she forgot, and woke to realize she had fallen asleep, confused for a second, fearing she was waking from the dream in Grampy's lap, and at the sight of the roof boards she felt years older from the girl who left two days ago on a Christmas trip to the Andrésons.

The moon was full, or as near to full as she could wish,

in its slow sail into silent sight out her window, far off yet near, with its weight of otherworldly substance. Mette swallowed hard as its glow appeared to pulse in time to the beat of her heart. The globe came to rest inside the circle of her window as she stared, as if her papa had fashioned the window to frame the moon in its path. This had happened exactly this way before and here it was again, so all will be well, she thought, and understood that her thought was thanks to God, and with that thought she was asleep.